AF278922

Medea
IN CORINTH

by

Brian Anderson

authorHOUSE®

AuthorHouse™
1663 Liberty Drive, Suite 200
Bloomington, IN 47403
www.authorhouse.com
Phone: 1-800-839-8640

First published by AuthorHouse   6/26/2008

ISBN: 978-1-4259-1227-7 (sc)

Printed in the United States of America
Bloomington, Indiana

This book is printed on acid-free paper.

Introductory Notes:
Medea and the Trans-Historical Situation of Greek Tragedy

Camus understood the power tragedy holds to enrapture and inspire readers and spectators of modern drama. Tragedy, he reminds us in the preface to *Caligula*, does not go in for the so-called "tricks" of the dramatic trade, such as labyrinthine plot structures, overtly bizarre character studies, risqué situations, and the use of superfluous, ornamental language. Tragedy needs none of these things, because its power lies in the straightforward communication of "human fate in all of its simplicity and grandeur." What could be more complex, confounding, and richly entertaining than this simplicity?

Although I have drawn great inspiration for this retelling from the ancient (Greek) and modern (French) poets, I have opted for a brisk, concentrated, and uncluttered reworking of the classic tragic tale, and have therefore deliberately avoided pretentious, unusual verbiage. My short tragic drama, *Medea in Corinth*, is presented without the formal use of poetic rhythm and meter. Instead, it employs colloquial language and common syntax in the style of free verse. The directness of the presentation is intended to enhance and intensify the emotional, psychological, and philosophical complexities of the story.

The adaptation of Greek tragedy for the new audience undoubtedly results from a moral response to the original play. Beyond the attempt to merely recreate an experience that we can only imagine (the relationship between the ancient dramatist and his audience at The Great Dionysia), this adaptation seeks to participate in the perennial discourse concerning issues that defy religious, scientific, and philosophical solutions.

Adaptation often takes a divergent path from that of the original when presenting its story, because its goal is to communicate, through interpretation and reinterpretation, the passionate and emotional qualities of the original while preserving the visceral and emotive gestures born of human pain, suffering and love, which always transcend the play's formal structure. For example, Jean Racine, in the *Phaedra*, steps beyond the structural boundaries of Euripides' *Hippolytus,* while retaining, and in many ways, surpassing the raw emotional fervor of the original work.

Medea is the classic instance of a scorned woman reacting violently to her husband's infidelity. Her terrible acts of brutality, infanticide being the most unsettling, although dreadful, were interpreted by the ancient Greeks as natural byproducts of the inevitable cycle of conflict and vindication at work within the cosmos. Many tragic-mythological characters from Greek antiquity are often portrayed as unwitting victims of fate. The inexplicable, sublime powers of nature ultimately overthrow them, for when oppressed and violated, the cosmic forces recoil, taking all things with them to destruction.

At most, Greek tragedy intimates philosophy's great debate concerning the problem of free will and determinism. Ancient drama records, for the first time in Athenian history, the embryonic stirring of the free will as an emerging human phenomenon. In Greek mythology, the heroes and heroines of antiquity are locked within a struggle for freedom against the superior forces of providential fate, as embodied in the archaic Greek goddess *Ananke,* who in myth, personified the unalterable law of necessity at work within the universe. *Ananke* was believed to govern both human and divine affairs with a power beyond the rule and justice of either *Themis* or *Dike.* Despite this understanding, the Greeks of the tragic age, focusing on the interrelationship between the human and divine, boldly questioned whether or not, and to what degree, they were captains of their own fate.

Tragedy deals with the fundamental situations within which we find ourselves as human beings. We all must die, suffer, and struggle against the world as subjects of chance and fate. These immutable truisms establish the existential parameters within which we define our human essence, shaping our possibilities and opening the realm of autonomous, decisive action. It has been shown, quite convincingly by Karl Jaspers, that without an understanding of the fundamental human situations, the full significance of our lives fails to manifest. Returning to the story of Medea, I move beyond the Greeks, a privilege afforded by the history of the times, in order to reexamine these fundamental situations anew, within the overarching context of an earthly existence devoid of providential fate as conceived by the ancients. The play focuses on the related issues of "anachronism" in social tradition (e.g., customs and religious belief), freedom of choice, and the ultimate moral responsibility of human action in a world estranged from divine sovereignty.

In Medea's case, social convention and orthodoxy were greatly responsible for the tragedy, so I look to the role of the woman in antiquity. However, as Bernard Knox quite correctly concludes in his study of Euripides' *Medea*, this play is not so much concerned with the issue of women's "rights," for more importantly it questions a woman's "wrongs" - those she sustains, and those she inflicts. The story is set in ancient Corinth, a colony of Greece, a male-dominated society where the search for self-meaning was often times lost amid gender metaphors and asymmetrical power struggles; Medea's world is eerily contemporary.

Medea's world was also a place where venerable tradition and the influence of religious superstition held sway; faith tended to dominate and override the more reasonable human sensibilities. Even the nascent science of the Presocratic philosophers, with its drive to understand the universe by means of rational inquiry and logical argument, tended to blur the contrast between myth and *logos*, or logic. Within their early philosophical attempts to explain natural phenomena, the line between inventive, creative explanations, and those of a more rational and analytic nature, was only beginning to be drawn. This is evident within the poetic cosmological speculation of such thinkers as Heraclitus, Parmenides, and Empedocles. As opposed to the later, more rigorous systematic thought of Plato and Aristotle, these early Greek thinkers philosophized through cryptic, oracular prose and elegantly structured poetry, which was in great part inspired by Greek religion. Their writings overflow with allusion and direct reference to the divine powers at work within the cosmos.

During the primordial Golden Age, the first age of the world, gods and humans coexisted in a blissful state, but with the great Promethean sacrifice, a fracture occurred, and the gaping chasm between mortals and divinity was established. The gods, through deception and persecution, established their superiority and divine right to power. This is what Hesiod tells us; this is the stuff of Greek myth. Such a history was very much alive to the Greeks during the age of the great tragic performances. At this time, they still shared a strong kinship with the mythic past, although they no longer actively worked to strengthen and perpetuate the relationship with the divine. The ritual of sacrifice, as opposed to displaying unwavering belief in and devotion to the Olympians and the pantheon of lesser deities, was for the most part practiced out of venerable obligation, within the atmosphere of celebration at the great festivals. In a critical sense, the Greeks slowly and methodically began to question their authentic relationship to the gods.

This is a time of critical import for the Greeks, a moment that required decisive action. For as the gods withdrew, or the importance of their presence diminished, humans had the option of either remaining indifferent to the their absence, or, with great concern, adopting a new stance toward their worldly existence. Without the pull and sway of the supernatural forces, the former ideas of fate and destiny called for reevaluation. In an era of great change, such concepts that previously held meaning in the mythological and archaic past, were exposed to the tribunal of logic, opened to a new form of critical and skeptical enquiry.

Perhaps Medea, much like tragedy itself, exists between two worlds: the archaic past, the age of myth, a life bound up with religious fate, and the emerging world of new values and sensibilities, developing in conjunction with the politics of the city-states and the nascent consciousness of moral culpability. As classicist Jean-Pierre Vernant convincingly argues, the tragic age is defined by the clash of these two worlds, which occurred as the language and symbol of myth was reassessed and reevaluated in a rational attempt to twist free from the constraining bonds of providence. When *mythos* ceased to have an indisputable stronghold on humanity, the potential for a new life strutted forward, taking a center stage within the dramas of the tragedians.

I chose against sanctioning Medea's actions with recourse to the gods, as an approval or censure of her unsettling and questionable actions (*deus ex machina*), in the manner of Euripides, Seneca, Corneille, and Anouilh. For example, although the French playwright Anouilh puts a modern twist on the conception of divine intervention by concluding his version of the drama with the suicide of Medea, it nonetheless begs the following question: Is this not simply another form of martyrdom with salvation, albeit of a secular kind, in that it categorically serves to justify her actions?

Rather, in the form of a paradigm shift, I envisage the players of *Medea in Corinth* entangled in the earthly struggle for selfhood and identity within a context resembling a modern crisis in faith, as prophesied so vehemently by Nietzsche. The moment God's death is descried, it strikes with full force, and earthly existence gets its most powerful and frightening impetus! When the universe is purged of intrinsic meaning and is no longer conceived in metaphysical or theological terms, the ephemeral and fragile nature of human existence is exposed for the first time in its long history. Our authentic existential situation, with its unique delimiting factors, is revealed: freedom arises and flourishes. The essence of our being human is thus laid bare in terms of our ultimate relation to death and radical finitude as divorced from providence.

As a point of interpretation, a somewhat modern conception of human fate as history, or destiny, is present to the pre-tragic literature of Greece, namely within the epic poetry of Homer's *Iliad,* where the individual's fate is seen as having a direct and profound effect on the destiny of a people. Achilles' life is understood as being influenced by fate, or *Ananke*; for it is determined by the gods that he shall live a short, but brilliant, life. Yet is such a life really given to him, or instead, is this the life that he ultimately chooses? The *Iliad* seems to insinuate the latter, and further, it suggests that human actions have a direct bearing on the society at large, and poor choices resulting from flawed deliberation and decision in the moment of action often produce unfavorable consequences, not only for the individual, but also for the society of which he is a part.

This Homeric notion of fate brings us closer to the existence of the modern human, as understood by the nineteenth and twentieth-century philosophers of existence than one might imagine. How is it that we come to "love our fate" in a world without intrinsic meaning, in a world where meaning must be created? When existence is liberated from religious determinism, the traditional ideas of fate, necessity, and destiny are open to a reinterpretation that reveals them as natural outgrowths of life's processes. As we struggle for freedom against our society, culture, and nature, amid random chance, the free choices we make become our fate, much like the fate of brave Achilles.

Perhaps it is true, as Sartre poetizes through the character of Orestes in *Les Mouches*, that human freedom begins when servitude to God ends. If so, this is the most burdensome of all liberations, because at the instant we are released from otherworldly aspirations and the restrictions of an absolutist, onto-theological world-view, an autonomy without excuse is thrust upon us, and we are, in Sartre's words, "condemned to be free." Thus, in terms of modern existentialism, this recovery of freedom violently throws us back upon our own resources. We are forced to acknowledge and accept the monumental task of assuming responsibility for our earthly being. Without recourse to God or some luminous realm of transcendent values, the consequences of our deeds fall squarely upon our shoulders, and in order to exist authentically, we must bear up this incredible weight with heroic resolve.

It is only within such an existence, divorced from God (and the gods), radically estranged from determinism, or providence, as hitherto conceived, that the question of what type of person commits the crime of infanticide, and why, assumes legitimate moral significance. Perhaps, in this day and age, we are better able to grasp the pressing immediacy and true moral weight of the question, but this does not guarantee that we are any better equipped than the ancient Greeks to provide the definitive answer.

Brian Anderson

Medea in Corinth:
A Tragedy in Five Episodes

Characters:

Medea: *The princess and sorceress of Cholchis and the daughter of King Aeetes. She is the legal wife of Jason.*

Jason: *Son of Aeson and rightful heir to the throne of Iolchus. He led the first European sailing expedition in search of the Golden Fleece aboard the vessel Argo.*

King Creon: *The ruler of Corinth and father to Creusa.*

Nurse: *Attendant and confidant to Medea who has traveled with her from Cholchis to Corinth.*

Pedagogue: *The tutor to the children of Jason and Medea.*

Hecate: *The ancient sorceress-goddess who travels the wooded groves with a band of ghosts and two large black hounds. She reigns over the three-fold domain of heaven, earth, and the underworld.*

Chorus: *The priestesses of Hecate.*

Corinthian Women: *The daughters, wives, and mothers of Corinth. They have taken sides with Medea during her divorce.*

Male children: *The young sons of Medea and Jason.*

Guardsmen: *A small unit of soldiers under the direct charge of King Creon.*

Prologue

(Lights up. Center stage. Two small children are seated. They laugh while playing a game. Enter Hecate bearing a torch and a spirit-wand. Three masks, bound with hemp, dangle from the tip of the stick she holds. Hecate smiles as she approaches and ushers the children off stage. She returns to deliver the prologue.)

Hecate:

I am Hecate, the tri-form goddess, mighty in heaven, on earth, and in the underworld, as beneficent as I am vindictive and malevolent when so provoked. I manifest to those who revere me by torch. My presence is most often felt at lonely crossroads. It is at such a juncture that we find Medea as the tale begins. Although the final act of the drama plays out here, in the sun-baked seaport of Corinth, the story began on the mainland, in the ancient region of Iolcus, born of a history inundated with great adventures, perilous tests of courage, and extraordinary feats of strength. In short, male games overwrought with deeds, lacking in thought. Jason, the son of Aeson, the great king of Iolchus in Thessaly, was on track to inherit the rule, until his evil uncle, Pelias, usurped the throne by way of deception and banished him from the court. Jason sought refuge with the wise, immortal centaur, Chiron, who taught him many and varied things including rhetoric, philosophy, and the art of warfare. Upon reaching manhood, Jason returned to Thessaly from exile to demand back his father's kingdom. Pelias, in a suspicious gesture, agreed to surrender Iolchus on the condition that Jason retrieve the legendary Golden Fleece, an ancient relic with magical powers. Pelias knew the fleece was in the possession of the cruel barbarian king Aeetes of Colchis. Within his custody, the golden idol was secured away in a temple and guarded by a monstrous, ever-vigilant serpent. It was for this endeavor, the retrieval of the Golden Fleece, that the first sailing vessel was constructed. It was called *Argo*, and manned by no less than fifty heroes, including Heracles, Orpheus, Castor, Pollux, Theseus, and their like. When the ship carrying Jason and the Argonauts reached Colchis, King Aeetes agreed to surrender the fleece under the condition that Jason carry out a series of dangerous labors. Aeetes challenged Jason to yoke a team of fire-breathing bulls in order to plow a massive field, sow it with dragon's teeth, and defeat the army of warriors that sprang from the soil. But, after Jason completed the labors, the king became angry, and decided not to relinquish the golden ram's skin. So, Jason and Medea hatched a plan to steal it. After lulling the watchful dragon to sleep with a powerful elixir, they swiped the Golden Fleece and sailed off. Soon after the theft, Aeetes lit out in fast pursuit. Working to halt her father's sailing fleet, Medea killed her brother, Aspyrtus, who was sailing along with the couple, and scattered his dismembered limbs over the sea. When Jason and Medea finally reached Iolcus, they were set to present Pelias with the Golden Fleece in exchange for the crown as promised. However, when they handed him the fleece, the king suddenly changed his mind and refused Jason the throne. Medea, once again, came to the aid of Jason, exacting just retribution for Pelias' treachery. She deceived the daughters of the aged Pelias into unwittingly murdering the old man. Promising that her powers of magic could secure eternal life for the king and his court, Medea convinced the girls to participate in a ritual sacrifice in which they sliced their father to bits and submerged his mutilated corpse into a vat of boiling oil. The subsequent hostility of Pelias' son, Acastus, who was enraged by the treachery of his father's murder, forced Jason and Medea to flee Iolcus. After much sailing, they eventually settled here, in Corinth, where they have lived happily, in a simple manner, for the last ten years, with their two sons.

(Pause)

Unfortunately, things have recently taken a turn for the worse. Jason's unrelenting obsession with nobility and status has driven him to the point of breaking his sacred marriage vows to Medea. So desperate is Jason's lust for a position of royalty, that he plans to abandon Medea in an attempt to secure a place of status within the kingdom of Corinth. To accomplish this end, he plans on seducing his way into the heart of Creusa, king Creon's lovely, young daughter.

> *(Hecate steps back. Enter the chorus of Priestesses who are led by Hecate.)*

Episode I

Choral Song:

Jason annuls the marriage to Medea, and scorns loyalty bound by the most intimate pledge, sworn eternal by the sacrosanct oath of Themis. He heaps torment upon innocent children with no thought for consequence. These acts are violent encroachments on Nature's order, established by the hallowed matriarchy of Night, Tethys, and Gaia, the great mothers of divine and human lineage. Even the thunder god holds these goddesses in reverence. Injustice must not be allowed to progress too far, or continue on for too long, lest order never be restored. By divine sanction, the fierce, retributive justice of Nemesis must follow, and all that lives should continue to pay reckoning until the equilibrium of the primeval world force is restored. Now, beneath the light and heat of Corinth's sun, the fateful destinies of Jason and Medea are at once, and for all eternity, linked.

> *(Stage to black. Lights up. Before Medea's house in Corinth, the Nurse sits outside speaking to the Pedagogue as Children play nearby.)*

Nurse:

I know and dread her wrath. She is terrible and dangerous if any rouse her hate. Oh, how happy we'd now be if the waves and rocks had crushed the accursed Argo in its quest to secure the Golden Fleece, before it reached the kingdom of Medea's father, Aeetes.

Pedagogue:

> *(Sullen)*

No one is happy. Perhaps fortunate and prosperous for a time, but never happy.

> *(Turns to look at the house.)*

Finally, her crying has ceased. Perhaps now we can have some peace.

Nurse:

For the moment she has collapsed in exhaustion, but when she recovers her strength the storm will continue, and mark my words, Poseidon himself could not unloose such a tempest.

Pedagogue:

Well, count her suffering double if what I heard is true. Poor woman, I fear her problems have only just begun.

Nurse:

Tell me, what is it?

Pedagogue:

Mind you, it's only a rumor, and I pray that it's false.

Nurse:

Out with it!

Pedagogue:

Oh, I never should have spoken…

Nurse:

I demand that you tell me at once, for I am her closest confidant!

Pedagogue:

Very well then. It is said that Creon has issued an edict banning Medea from Corinth, and not only her, but the children, too. However, once again, I remind you that it's only a rumor.

Nurse:

Although Jason spurns Medea, treating her worse than a dog, surely he'll protect the children…

Pedagogue:

> A throne, nubile young bride, and new offspring…
> so tempting are such things.
>
> *(Sarcastically)*
>
> Now the glory of Aeson's house lives on with honor. But is any man different? Look, there in the distance, the wedding festival for Jason and Creusa. The torches of the Corinthians burn, like Jason's new love, with hot intensity, while the brilliance of the flame he once carried for Medea now dims.

Nurse:

> Vile ingrate! No Greek-born woman could have made a better wife to Jason than Medea. She dedicated herself to him heart and soul, doing his bidding and dirty work, while severing her family ties. She fought and murdered in order to save his miserable life! It is said that Hera favors Jason. She is thought to have persuaded Aphrodite to induce Medea to fall head over heels in love with Jason. And how fortunate for him indeed! Her beauty rivals that of any of the goddesses, and she as well possesses an intellect of the first order. I tell you truly, Medea can match wits with any man in debate! She is also an expert in the use of herbal poisons, spells, and remedies. Such powers are at her disposal as niece to Circe! Remember, that it was Medea who provided the supernatural means

by which Jason mastered the bulls and earth-born soldiers of Aeetes. Honoring his request, she has ceased working her magic spells. She has not buried a single curse tablet since landing in Corinth.

(Pause)

I recall the day when they joined hands and invoked the gods in the most sacred of all time-honored pledges - the vow of marriage! Now she lies grieving and fasting, her body wasted through tears that continually fall. Dishonored, she'll receive no recompense from Jason!

Pedagogue:

Oh, the sacrifices one makes for love.

> *(Pedagogue leads the children*
> *into the house.)*

Nurse:

Look at those beautiful children born of their union. How I long to tell the children what kind of man they have for a father – master or not – he should die, or worse!

> *(Nurse to Pedagogue)*

Hey, keep those babes from their mother's sight, do you hear? And say nothing of the decree.

> *(Interior of Medea's house. She*
> *is in a rage.)*

Medea:

> Get them out of my way! They are spawns of a hateful father and hated mother! May this accursed house be razed to the ground and fall in ruins! Oh, if only death would end this living hell and I would be through with it all. No…
>
> > *(Medea reaches to embrace the children.)*
>
> Come here. I do not hate you.
>
> > *(Medea pulls back from the children.)*
>
> Oh, Hera, great daughter of Rhea, your own divine suffering is mirrored in my mortal predicament. Recall when Zeus egregiously mistreated you! Mercilessly beaten, you were cast from your heavenly dwelling while cold fetters of adamantine secured your arms and a great weight strapped to your ankles drew you earthward.
>
> In agony and humiliation, you were stretched between the time of the immortals and humanity. Oh, Hera, your powerful oath of marriage, consecrated in the presence of Themis, no longer binds Jason to me. I implore your holy pity and compassion, for you, of all goddesses, should best relate to my feelings and motives. Much like you, I suffer at the hands of a male, I experience the brand of pain and torment that only a woman knows!

Pedagogue:

> My lady, excuse me, you have visitors. Strangers from Corinth – women of Corinth – should I send them away and tell them to return at a later time?

Medea:

> Strangers you call them? You have unwittingly hit upon a cuttingly harsh reality. For even here, in the land of their birth, these Corinthian women *are* "strangers," exiles without home of identity, separated from the processes of law and those who execute them. Thus, am I not doubly estranged? Remember, my dear Pedagogue, I came to Corinth as a foreigner and outcast, I am the stranger.

Pedagogue:

> No, you are never an outcast! You are the beautiful and powerful princess and sorceress of Colchis!

Medea:

> I am now a princess without a kingdom and a sorceress estranged from divine Nature, the inexhaustible well-spring of all life and vitality. It's been ten years since I've paid ceremonial tribute to great Mother Gaia.

Pedagogue:

> I'm sorry to have disturbed you, my lady. It is obvious that company at such a time would only pose an imposition. I'll send them away.

Medea:

> No, we must be hospitable and kind to our friends. Let's greet them. After you show them in, please put out the wine and nourishment.
>
> > *(Enter Four Corinthian Women, linen chitons with himations drawn over their heads. The Pedagogue sets out the krater of wine and small cakes of grain. Enter the Nurse, who begins to ladle wine into the drinking cups of earthenware. The women sit around a short table.)*

Woman #1:

> We are the women of Corinth and have just returned from the wedding celebration for Jason and Creusa. Upon hearing your story, we were greatly saddened. Lady Medea, with all respect I say...

Woman #2:

> *(Interrupting)*
>
> No, we say – no man is worth such suffering.

Medea:

> Good ladies, I cannot feign my happiness, for without my husband Jason no joy lives within

these accursed walls. Oh, what can I say, I am in love with the most loathsome of all men!

(Pause)

My apologies, I fear that I may confirm the rumors and prove myself an inadequate and unsociable hostess.

Woman #1:

Fret not Medea, we are all mothers, daughters, widows, and divorcees. We've been through it all, to hell and back, and know a woman's life can be difficult.

Woman #2:

Mocked by the gods, we are the unhappiest creatures of all.

Nurse:

I spit on a woman's lot and curse those barbaric males who seek to reign sovereign over our bodies and souls!

(The Pedagogue exits nervously.)

Medea:

You said it! Men possess the dominant upper hand. And not just in Greece and Corinth, but elsewhere too. Our fathers purchase our husbands with the dowry, not the man of our dreams, you understand, but someone our male relatives deem the proper consort. And what if he turns out a rogue? Well, you can forget about divorce. In essence, a tyrant is bought to rule and beat us down.

Woman #3:

We are married as witless girls, youths, child-brides all...

Nurse:

...You mean babies!

(Laughter)

Medea:

Yes, and then we are expected to accomplish the impossible and divine what pleases a man in all aspects. Why? Because we have not learnt it at home, and we certainly can't hope for meaningful discourse with our husbands. If we fail in the bedroom - whores, concubines, and slaves are more than eager to provide the company to wipe away his despondency!

Woman #2:

We must look only to the man for our companionship, while he regularly seeks company elsewhere.

Medea:

(Mockingly)

That's because he's searching out a higher, deeper intellectual union than we're capable of providing. So off he goes chasing little boys around the gymnasium.

(Laughter)

Woman #1:

...Better home than out in public.

Medea:

Honorable, they say, to neither be seen nor heard. That is best! We are safely locked away in our squalid, unclean quarters, spinning and weaving, while they are abroad fighting wars in our defense! In all truth, three times would I rather stand in the front line of battle than to once endure childbirth.

(Women indicate agreement.)

Woman #3:

Our situations indeed appear bleak, but what of yours, Medea? Your pain must be far more intense.

Medea:

It is true. I am forlorn and city-less, hated by my husband. I have no kin left. No mother, brother, or father exists to provide me a safe haven from this storm of troubles.

Woman #1:

Poor Medea, how can we help you?

Medea:

Please, not your pity, anything but that. Perhaps, there is a favor I would ask of you, because there's something upon which I've been deliberating... I've been hatching a plot.

(Medea rises.)

If I find some way to retaliate and punish my husband for these cruel wrongs he has suffered me. I entreat that you reveal nothing whatsoever of what I've told you.

(Pause)

Oh, I am tormented concerning what seems the inevitability of my revenge, and the course it should ultimately take. But, whatever manner of retaliation I ultimately choose to thwart my enemies, no one should betray me and speak of it.

Nurse:

Vengeful wrath in a stealthy, well-devised plan always has the element of surprise as its greatest ally.

Woman #3:

> You have our loyalty. We vow to keep silent. We will not betray your trust.

>> *(The sound of Creon and the royal guardsmen approaching interrupts the conversation. The Women are silent and all look to the door.)*

Nurse:

> The pedagogue was right! Creon and the royal soldiers are descending on the house!

Woman #1:

> Medea, our king seeks you out.

Medea:

>> *(Reaching out her hands to the Women)*

> You have all made good company for me. I thank you.

Episode II

Choral Song:

Creon, the earthly king-god, swollen with lordship, now descends upon the house. He, like Zeus, rules through the exercise of brute strength, the very opposite of cunning, recklessly wielding power to defeat and subjugate all enemies. Long before Pandora's appearance, a patriarchal reign was established high upon Olympus, where the fear of violence sealed bonds of holy union. But the gods' need to strike terror in women, is a response to their own fear and hatred of our secrets, for we hold the key to the mysteries of the universe, and in strength and intellect, will prove superior, self-sufficient beings. And whilst this godly rule is a grave injustice, to dare raise a hand against this ancient, venerable tradition would inflame their wrath, begging destruction!

> *(Medea steps out of the house.*
> *The Women follow her out.*

*Creon moves between the armed
guardsmen toward Medea.)*

Creon:

Medea, go now from Corinth in exile and take
your two brats with you! I have so decreed it! If
not for Jason, your dark and dangerous plague
would have been eradicated by force of arms! You
owe him a great debt of gratitude, for he strongly
lobbied to spare your worthless life. Your safety
here in Corinth is no longer guaranteed, so flee my
kingdom and spread the seeds of your infectious
poison elsewhere. Be on your way!

*(Medea aggressively charges
Creon and the Soldiers.)*

Medea:

What's the charge?

Creon:

Stay back, you vile witch! Curb your irreverent
tongue in the presence of your king! Only an
innocent woman should ask such a question. Tell
me, did old Pelias have a hearing?

(Pause)

And when you turned like a tigress on your own
brother, your own flesh and blood, did he have a
say-so? Oh, such black and treacherous deeds you
have committed, you're a thief and a murderer!

32

Medea:

> When you speak of the theft of the Golden Fleece,
> the murder of Aspyrtus and Pelias, know well
> that the promised bridegroom, your future son-
> in-law, was with me every step of the way. I did
> not commit these black and treacherous deeds
> alone. Murder was committed in the name of
> Jason; thus he shares the guilt as a co-conspirator
> in these crimes.

Creon:

> No, you alone are responsible for the lengthy list
> of odious sins. Jason can mount a logical defense
> to stave off guilt, but this cannot be said of you.
> You're a clever and cunning woman, and your
> skill in the black arts, as taught to you by Circe
> and Hecate, as is well known. Truth be told,
> Medea, I fear you and so do the good citizens
> of Corinth …and for good reason, you've hurled
> vicious threats against my family, and my only
> daughter!

Medea:

> Sire, my reputation continues to wrongly oppress
> me.

Creon:

> No, I think not. You've lost your husband and now
> with the brute strength of a man you demonstrate
> a woman's passionate and irresponsible behavior.

I can perhaps tolerate mild doses of arrogance in a male, but when a woman flaunts such haughty pride, I despise it! Teetering on the brink of madness, you've no thought for what is best in this situation, and I want you nowhere near Corinth when you fly off the edge.

Medea:

"Evil foreigner," "sorceress," and above all "clever woman!" Admit that it's my intelligence, above all else, that you dread and abhor. As a woman, my sharp intellect brands me a criminal!

(Pause)

But, how smart can I really be? Look at the predicament I now find myself in! Could not the high priestess of Hecate work black magic to win over Jason, enthralling and bewitching him back into love? Why then does he seek to marry your daughter? Answer me that.

(Pause)

I recall when the rays of Helios, my divine grandfather, the source of all human vision, emanated from my very being. At that time, nobles competed for my hand in marriage, but now, alas, the tables have turned – from royalty to exile. Fear me not, king, considering that you have done me no wrong. It is Jason, my worthless husband, who angers me. Not only does he want me out of the house to make official the divorce, beyond this, he wants to see me banished from the country, but he can't find the courage to face me. So, he hides behind regal purple, and sends a king to do his bidding.

Creon:

Know that it is with the safety of Creusa that I am concerned. This above and beyond any kingly obligation makes it imperative that my ruling of exile be upheld. Now take your lethal potions and release my kingdom from the stronghold of your hellish terror!

Medea:

Do not fear me; I will not harm your home. Why should I hate you when you only seek to protect the one you love, as any righteous man would? Jason should take lessons from you. Please, let me stay even if in some far-removed portion of your land where I can humbly raise my children. I am broken and I beg on the life of your daughter – has all sense of pity left you?

Creon:

My love for Creusa far exceeds the limits of pity! Medea, your words are now gentle and carry the rational tone of a Greek.

(Pause)

But, far more do I trust the wild, barbarian side you've shown.

Medea: *(Weeping)*

Oh, love hurts! Never would I wish it on my most hated enemies.

Creon:

Enough of this dialogue! Never will you sway me! My decree of exile stands. If you have not cleared the Isthmus by tomorrow's sunrise, I will be compelled to use force.

Medea:

So be it, I swear by Themis to uphold your declaration: I will go. However, before departure, may I ask one favor of you?

Creon:

Speak.

Medea:

I pray, please allow a brief respite before the punishment commences. Grant me one day longer in order to collect my meager store of belongings and make ready the children. At least show pity to them. Forget about me and imagine instead your child. Please see it in your heart to weep for my children who are now destined to learn the hard way the meaning of grief!

Creon:

Medea, there is no easy way to learn of life's terrible truths, a hard and fast lesson is by far the best. However, I'm neither a heartless despot nor barbarian. Never have I exercised my power in a reckless, tyrannical manner. I am not a king who revels in trampling on the less fortunate and rejoicing in their calamity. Quite the contrary, I am a ruler who embraces his royal birthright as a privilege.

(Long pause)

So be it, I grant you this one last day, but if tomorrow finds the three of you here...

Medea:

Bless you, and bless the royal marriage, and your hopes for the future prosperity of your kingdom. You have adjudicated wisely today. You demonstrate the glorious power in possession of kings, in that you're a just man. I do not begrudge your happiness.

Creon:

Promise me, Medea, that I won't come to regret this gesture of compassion.

> *(Creon exits with guardsmen as
> Medea turns to the Women.)*

Woman #1:

One day of reprieve seems utterly useless. Poor Medea, overcome by the wild, pathless waves of bad fortune.

Medea:

> It appears that way, but I have a plan, so don't worry. Do you think I would fawn on such a creature except with guileful intent to profit? Now shall all three regret this day!
>
> > *(Interior of house. Medea paces the floor as the nurse looks on.)*

Nurse:

> I feared this moment.

Medea:

> How can I tolerate the injustice of such oppressive treatment without vengeance? Let weaker women be praised for their muted virtue. Silence and passivity sanction atrocity! To hell with Creon and Jason, and to hell with what the poets teach. If Phoebus Apollo had the good sense to bestow upon women the gift of song, how different the music and lyrics would be. I will not be remembered as a member of the weaker sex!

Nurse:

> Medea, I know this is no ordinary crime you are planning. I see something monstrously inhumane and godless! You will outdo yourself, won't you, even at the expense of your own safety? Your reason is now goaded by anger. Please, I beg of you, master your heart with a sound mind and quell your wild spirit!

Medea:

> I can be quiet only when I see everything overwhelmed, even if it means my own ruin! Oh, so many ways of killing, but which one to select? Fire? Yes, I see them burning in flames unquenchable, with their flesh bubbling and melting from the bone as they collapse into charred smoldering heaps. Or, perhaps, a well-whetted sword driven deep into the stomach. Wait, but what if the guardsmen capture me while I'm torching the house or running them through? Surely I will be killed amid the cruel laughter of those who hate me. No, I cannot allow myself to be mocked, not even in death.

Nurse:

> *(Interrupting)*
>
> Be careful, I say, no one can attack such a kingdom and topple a long-standing reign of power!

Medea:

> What you really mean to say is that no woman is up to the task! Well I am! From this day forward, let men tremble in fear when they speak of me! The name of Medea will soon be spoken of loudest and my actions shall bear witness to my cunning and courage.

Nurse:

> Medea, you must set limits…

Medea:

> Don't talk to me of limits, moderation, and temperance!

Nurse:

> Excessive behavior always paves the way for disastrous consequences.

Medea:

> *(Composed)*

> Answer me this, what limits should one realistically place on love?

Nurse:

> *(Silent)*

Medea:

> Well, then, let the same restrictions apply to hatred.

> *(Turns from Nurse)*

> Now, back to the plan…Poison, yes, poison! As niece to the most infamous sorceress and witch, Circe, this is where my talent lies! I'll mix a lethal blend that will induce seizures – they'll drop amid paroxysms, and their muscles will spastically cramp with such force as to snap their bones. Such a macabre delight to imagine them writhing in agony before they die…

Episode III

Choral Song:

Now shall womanhood be ennobled. The slanderous tongues of the poets shall cease in wrongly assailing us. The male race shall be exposed as a murdering, deceitful, and savage race. Those who desecrated the solemn oaths will now pay the supreme penalty for these crimes. The cycle of violence turns on itself, changing Nature's order, reversing her laws. Rivers flow uphill, treams are sucked up back to their source. As an answer to the fury of the male, the hymn of Medea we now uplift for time to record no more the passive suppliant, but an aggressive force as terrible as anything that Nature has yet unleashed. The new Typhoeus, springing from Gaia's fertile womb, thus is Medea!

> *(A loud knock interrupts Medea as she speaks. The Pedagogue looks to Medea then moves to the portico.)*

Pedagogue:

Who could that be? Who's there?

> *(Enter Jason. He violently pushes the Pedagogue to the ground. Medea, incensed, confronts him.)*

Jason:

Hurling threats at the king, have you lost all sense? Medea, your arrogant pride continues to work against you. You simply can't restrain your lawless tongue! Count it merciful that you are still alive. Creon was set on execution, and I softened his wrath with tears and choice words. I prevailed upon him to banish you instead.

Medea:

And I thought ostracism a punishment. But, your well-worded rationalization renders it far more favorable.

> *(Pause)*

Remove me from the premises and you have your common-law divorce - or should I say have Creon remove me? Again, someone else fights the battle for you! Jason, you're shameless!

Jason:

I saved your life!

Medea:

And how many times have I saved yours? Every Greek on the *Argo* knows that I taught you to tame the fire-breathing bulls, helped you destroy Aeetes' soldiers, sown from dragon's teeth.

Jason:

To golden Aphrodite alone do I owe my safe voyage.

Medea:

Remember, that we heisted the golden religious fetish, only after I drugged the dragon with magic herbs. Two kingdoms were destroyed because of the wrongs you suffered, a brother and an old king murdered. And after all this, you toss me aside for another woman, and in doing so you shatter a faith in the holiest of bonds. Let Themis forever bear witness to this atrocity!

Jason:

What convoluted nonsense! Should I be guilty of these crimes? They're your crimes – the crimes of Eros, for you contrived all of your scheming under love's spell, intoxicated by the arrow of Eros shot from his bow.

Medea:

Our attraction should be attributed to the unholy spell of the black Aphrodite of Cyprus! Lust for your body perhaps, but certainly not your heart, or way of thought.

(Pause)

Jason, I tell you truly that those who profit by a crime must own up to the guilt! They are indeed your crimes!

Jason:

(Reflective pause)

Yet, despite it all, in the end, Medea, you have certainly gained far more than you ever gave or sacrificed.

Medea:

Your smug Greek maleness befouls the thought process! This I've got to hear.

Jason:

As opposed to the barbarian land of Colchis, you're living in glorious Greece, and surrounded by a learned, just, and civilized culture. Through my achievements aboard the *Argo*, your name will forever be spoken throughout the ages. You will have immortal fame.

(Medea laughs.)

If you could only see that my marriage to Creusa will be of great benefit to everyone. We too shall prosper. After the murder of Pelias, what was I to do? Remember, I am on the run too, as an exile.

So, what better way to protect you, our children, and myself than marrying the king's daughter? I don't hate you nor do I lust for another bride. I can see that the princess's charms provoke your jealousy, but it's not about the bed, I tell you.

Medea:

But you will produce new offspring with her, right?

(Long pause)

I gave you two healthy children, two beautiful male children!

Jason:

Believe me, I love our boys, and have no complaints. However, our poverty is an embarrassment, and with this I take issue, as it wins no friends and brings only shame. You must understand that I am born of a kingly lineage. We are now vagrants and outcasts, forever wandering, on the run. Such a lifestyle does not suit me well. I want to secure a better life, that is, a better life for both of us. So, why not royal brothers for our sons? This way, we might all live on in distinction, happiness, and most of all, prosperity.

Medea:

Oh, such clever arguments you construct. Jason, you're a rhetorician pure and simple, twisting and manipulating words, constructing what you believe to be clever arguments in your defense. Well, your case is pathetic, and your words are devoid of truth! You once claimed to fear and detest the power that accompanies the king's reign, I now know, to the contrary, that you actually desire such power! Once again, your judgment conflicts with mine. By the heavens, I pray to always possess the wisdom to shun fortunes. It sickens me to see how desperate you are for a royal lineage!

Jason:

If only you did possess real wisdom. Then you'd know good fortune from bad. I tell you again, I do not love her, but will wed her to strengthen our house, to help our children – to help you!

Medea:

(Weeping)

Go back to your virgin bride and away from the destitute foreign wife who shames you. You have stayed too long from Creusa's supple young limbs.

Jason:

You must listen…

Medea:

Do you remember how many times you clasped my knees as suppliant in Cholcis and Iolchus, and spread them as lover? This right hand you held in a pledge of undying faith…

(Medea and Jason kiss.)

Humor me, and for the sake of old times, remember fondly what we once meant to each another.

Jason:

(Silent)

Medea:

Listen to me, Jason…

Jason:

Medea, tell me what it is I can do to ease your burden?

Medea:

(Smiling)

Let's take to the seas again and continue our adventures as husband and wife!

Jason:

Have you forgotten our enemies? Do you ever grow tired of tempting Fate?

Medea:

(Laughing)

No! Even Fate herself stands inferior to me!

Jason:

Perhaps, it is with our earthly foes that you should concern yourself. Recall that Acastus is still on the hunt, and if we run, we'll surely make an enemy of Creon, who will undoubtedly become our most feared adversary. And what if Acastus and Creon unite, and take up arms against us?

Medea:

I'm not suggesting that we take up arms against these fearful opponents. I'm simply suggesting that we flee Corinth, and free ourselves from guilt's oppression.

Jason:

Medea, wait...

Medea:

Run with me, Jason, we'll set sail at day's break. My grandfather's golden torch will light the way for our escape.

Jason:

(Angered)

Medea, you must listen! Ask yourself seriously, what chance is there of safely escaping?

(Pause)

Enough already, let's cut this reunion short, or suspicions will be aroused.

Medea:

> (*Silent*)

Jason:

> Medea, please listen...

Medea:

> I'm unwise, what can I say? We women are no more than we are – women. Never attempt to either match us in malice or stoop to our low level of folly.
>
> > (*As if resigned to the inevitable*)
>
> What must be will be.

Jason:

> Can I now praise this new attitude, or will it change?
>
> > (*Smiling*)
>
> Seriously, if I can provide reasonable consolation from my father-in-law's house, ask it.

Medea:

> All I desire is that you allow me to take the children to accompany me in exile so that I may pour my tears upon them. You can expect new sons.

Jason:

No, my paternal obligation forbids such a request. Not even the king can drive me to abandon my boys. They are my reason for living, and they alone bring comfort to my soul grown weary of a burdensome existence. I would rather be deprived of light, limbs, and life than surrender my children.

> *(Medea pulls away from Jason and calls to the Pedagogue. She claps three times and the Children with the Pedagogue appear. Medea speaks in a hurried, somewhat unnatural tone.)*

Medea:

Come, boys, we are friends once again. Speak to your father – be reconciled – our peace has been made and no anger is left. Plans have changed: you are to stay with your father.

Jason:

The past is now absolved of blame and guilt, I forgive you. How can I hold you responsible for being a woman? It's only natural for a wife to lose her head and lash out in a situation such as this.

Medea:

I am suddenly overcome by the dread of foreboding. I tremble at the dangers still lurking ahead for our children.

Jason:

Don't worry, I will protect them. I give you my word.

(To the children)

You will both be honored in Corinth. Thanks to the gods, you will triumph in manhood over your father's enemies.

(To Medea)

What's wrong?

Medea:

Oh, it's nothing. I am only concerned for the children. So weak am I, so easily given over to tears. It's just that Creon was adamant about their exile and threatened to kill all three of us if we did not take flight by morning's light.

Jason:

Yes, I know. He must be plied and softened in some way. I have accomplished this once already, surely I can do it again. Medea, you of all people should know how persuasive I can be.

Medea:

> I have it! You must go by way of Creusa for this favor. Creon so loves his little girl that he will go to any lengths to please her. You ply her with the sweet talk and then…
>
> *(Pause)*
>
> But wait, think of how much more leverage we'll have if I send along with you a peace offering, gifts beyond Creusa's wildest comprehension – a glorious, flowing dress made of the most delicate and glowing fabrics, a tiara of gold to crown her flowing curls. Imagine how blessed she will feel when her promised bridegroom presents her with gifts laden with priceless jewels from the house of the sun god Helios.

Jason:

> *(Smirking)*
>
> More than gifts, Creusa will prize my words. The palace does not lack in anything – Why should a queen be smitten by gifts from your store? I don't know about this.

Medea:

> Is she a woman? Then gifts will persuade her. Oh, you still have much to learn about us, Jason.

Jason:

> Medea, please keep these heirlooms for yourself,
> they were a wedding gift from your father.

Medea:

> I'm begging you, allow me to do this for the
> children.

Jason:

> You're impossible! I give up. You wear me down.
> Very well then, if this is what you want.

Medea:

> You go along ahead and I will ready the gifts and
> send them with the boys. When she looks in their
> eyes she will melt, this I promise you!
>
> > *(Exit Jason. He leaves the house
> > and heads to Corinth and the
> > palace of Creon. Looking back,
> > he shouts to Medea.)*

Jason:

> Medea, truly do I applaud this new outlook.
> You are clever beyond the limitations of your race
> and sex.
>
> > *(The Nurse and Corinthian
> > Women stand nearby.)*

Medea:

> Pedagogue, take the children outside. Go!

> *(Medea moves to the center of the house.)*

When I am through with Jason, he will wish for a quick death.

> *(Turns to the Nurse)*

You are my most trusted and loyal confidant, assist me now as my scheme unfolds. Fetch me the sacred heirlooms of my divine ancient heritage: Bring the dress, presented to me by my father, Aeetes, the beaded necklace with medallions cast in gold, and last, the tiara, inlaid with precious stones from the Cyclades. These things my sons will take as gifts to the ill-fated bride, but first, I will soak them in poison. Come, we now invoke Hecate. Set up the tripods, prepare the lethal rights, and pray that my ties to the heavens are once more restored.

> *(The Nurse fetches the tripod. The Nurse and Women huddle together. Medea kneels between the posts and opens her casket of herbs, roots, and potions.)*

Nurse:

> *(In a hushed tone)*

Great destruction looms near. A wilder Medea than this I have never seen!

Corinthian Women:

There is no force in the universe as volatile and malevolent as a wife's rage when she is deprived of her husband.

Nurse:

(In a hushed tone)

She now unwraps her deadly stash of narcotics, and with left hand, conjures forth her witchery. Mixing the death-dealing herbs, she invokes the powers of the netherworld.

(Medea kneels before the altar and unwraps her herbs. She mixes an elixir and drinks it down.)

Medea:

Hecate, descendent of eternal Night, and daughter of Perses and Asteria, I offer you these solemn rights, and pray that you answer my cries of injustice just as you once responded to the urgent call of Persephone. Jason is no less an offense against Nature's sacred order than Hades, who abducted and cruelly raped the fair daughter of Demeter. Oh, great goddess of the moon and nocturnal hunt, I beckon you forth in three deadly forms to exact revenge. For you, I utter the incantations of the secret rites of Aegina, where flames from the sacrificial altar of the black ram illume the shores of the Saronic Gulf. For you, after my lineage of witches, I unloose my hair and dance bare-footed in the dark, mystic grove of Avernus. Hear now my petitions as I invoke your aid!

> *(Thunder sounds, lightning flashes, and the harsh sound of dog's bark is audible.)*

Nature's sublime powers, at the command of Hecate, now rumble my altars! My prayers have been received! Oh, bless you, bless you, strong, three-fold sorceress!

> *(The voice of Hecate resonates off stage.)*

Hecate:

Medea, most devoted of my priestesses, I now come to you.

> *(In a trance, Medea, rises. Enter Hecate who walks to Medea.)*

Hecate:

Remember, things do not always right themselves without causing harm. Heavy rains that end a drought can, in turn, inflict great destruction, for in the eternal cycle, the dry pays wet retribution. You believe that heaven's law has been violated, and that its proper balance must be restored through divine intervention…You envisage yourself, as high priestess, acting as the divine intermediary for Nemesis, who sends down her cosmic justice to eradicate the forces, which have upset the natural order of things by overstepping their prescribed boundaries.

Medea:

Yes, yes! Oh, dear Hecate, let me be the agent of the goddesses, as punishment is meted out in order to rectify the wrongs of the world.

Hecate:

Listen carefully to my words. You see vengeance as an instrument of the goddesses, but do you really know what it is to be divine, to live the eternal life of an immortal? In order to dwell as one of us you must relinquish all of your ties to earthly relations. To become immortal you must become something other than mortal, other than human—*you must become inhuman*! To emblazon in flames the name of "Medea" across the midnight sky for all eternity, to brand your fame into the collective minds and souls of future generations you must die to womanhood!

Medea:

Yes, in the company of the great goddesses! As the fate of the universe hangs in the balance, we now conspire to set the cosmos back on its rightful course, inverting the order by overturning the reign of the phallus!

Hecate:

In working to eradicate Jason's new kingly line, you seek to destroy a king's offspring, and more, bring down Corinth's royal house. Medea, with these acts, begins your separation from humanity. When this process is complete, you shall have immortality, and this, of course, comes with a high price. What has been familiar must become foreign, there must be a death to the old certainties. The wife, priestess, and mother, all these things, and more, you must kill in order that you might live forever! But, can you expect to exist beyond time, without such a sacrifice? To live now is to die to the old ways and be reborn in the company of the immortals. I tell you now, if you so choose, eternity is yours for the taking, and in the name of Medea, shall you live forever! However, you must think not of Dike, Nemesis, or Themis, for vengeance will be in your name!

Medea:

The rule of all law is that injustice should not continue for too long. Those who push the boundaries with violence and insolence must be marked for retribution.They must be engaged with equal or superior fury. Hecate, I accept the monumental responsibility of the task that you have entrusted to me, along with the destiny that bears my name. I now see, to be in the company of the divine requires a great sacrifice, for I must offer up the world. Thus, as you have decreed, in the name of Medea, justice will be exacted!

> *(Hecate exits, leaving Medea alone. Hecate whispers from off stage.)*

Hecate:

In the name of MEDEA...

> *(Medea lies sprawled on the floor of her house and the Nurse and Pedagogue are crouched beside her.)*

Nurse:

> *(Shaking Medea awake)*

Medea, Medea!

Medea:

> *(Grinning in a macabre manner)*

Unlike the stone at Delphi, foretelling of human fate in riddled obscurity, Hecate spoke to me, and did so directly. I am once again privileged among humans, and will soon be honored in the company of the great goddesses. United with the ancient earthly powers of Night, Thetis, and Gaia, my powers have returned. The flames of Hecate's torch burn within, I've been transformed.

(Wild-eyed)

I am called upon to carry out a great task, womanhood, and more, the fate of the entire universe rests upon my shoulders, hinges on my actions.

(Pause)

Did you see her in all of her magnificence?

Nurse:

Medea, you're hallucinating! We are the only ones here with you. Hecate did not, as you believe, manifest her presence.

Medea:

That's utterly impossible!

> *(Rising, ignoring the Nurse, Medea moves to the altar and removes a small jeweled dagger from its sheath.)*

I conjure the deities of the dead. Ghosts, I command you to leave your dwellings and torments. Fly like noxious winged Harpies, and descend upon the new marriage with hooked beaks open and talons spread. Foil Jason's plans to perpetuate the phallic order, and destroy the vessel that he hopes will carry his seed to fertility! No royal lineage shall there be. Death to the bride. And now, with a single cut of the ritual dagger, I supply life's hallowed liquid to fuel the torches.

> *(Medea cuts herself with the dagger and drips blood into the flame. The fire surges.)*

Marvel as the flames of Night thrust their blaze skyward!

> *(Medea reaches for the garments and raises them above her head.)*

Tinge Creusa's robe with my poison, Hecate. Protect and nurture the seeds of evil I plant within the cloth.

> *(Medea spills the poisonous liquid from the flasks and vessels upon the dress.)*

Pedagogue, bring my sons here at once!

> *(Medea's sons are led in by the Pedagogue.)*

Go, my sons, the mother who gave birth to you asks that you now placate your new mother with humble prayers and presents. March off now, and come back quickly so that we may share one last moment together, one last kiss and embrace before I am ostracized from this land, but not by means of any earthly king's judgment will my exile occur, but rather by the decree of a law whose authority is sanctioned by a power beyond even the mightiest of gods.

(Children leave with Pedagogue carrying the robes.)

Episode IV

Choral Song:

No hope exists for the ill-fated Creusa. Soon the maiden will receive her gifts. And she will adorn her fair locks with the wreath of death. Yet she is no innocent within this drama, and a most deserving casualty of divine recompense. Creusa is no less an effrontery to womanhood than Hypermnestra, the ancient criminal and traitor, who refused to align herself with her sisters when they rightly buried the forty-nine daggers in the backs of their male oppressors on the eve of the wedding nuptials. Jason, the vile, wretched soul, shall experience the torturing anguish of death, the palace of Corinth shall be the dwelling of Thanatos, as his own children bring doom and destruction. This day, Medea deals a swift, rightly deserved blow to Jason. Now we witness his fall!

(Interior of Medea's house.)

Medea:

> I am anything but a poor indefensible woman and wife. I am a different breed of woman cut from a different stock. I am kind to my friends, but a vengeful fury to those who wrong me, and only is such a person worthy of glory! I was cursed the day that guileful Greek lured me from my father's island kingdom, but he will pay for what he has suffered me. I shall now triumph at last as my hated enemies fall to the sacrosanct hands of vengeance. At this very instant, the robe and crown bathed in poison is killing the bride. The house of Jason shall crumble in ruins!
>
> But what of my children, now that they have been drawn into this web of brutality? Destined into it, it would almost seem, yet this was unclear from Hecate's communication.

> *(Pause)*

> Kinsmen of the slain will surely avenge their loss on the children. In madness, Creon's kingdom will stalk and slaughter them, and I fear that not even sanctuary in the sacred temple of Hera will put off a mob overcome with bloodlust!
>
> And what of their fates if they manage to escape? I imagine a dire endowment for my poor children. They'll be forced to live on the run as outcasts, banished beyond the city limits, hunted as if wild beasts! Should they grow up to be despised and ridiculed, forever estranged from their true home?

Those holding the scales, who judge me without hearing or trial, will also condemn my boys with extreme prejudice. As they grow, the children will carry the shameful burden of guilt, the guilt of a mother wrongly accused. Neither child will dare raise his eyes for fear of scorn. I pity them both, and never was a mother's concern more justified. How can I, with good conscience, expose them to such a violent fate? As a merciful mother, filled to overflow with love for her children, it tortures me to imagine such a depressing, impoverished existence for my boys.

Rather than this, I would see them devoured by flames from heaven!

Horror has rocked me and my limbs fall numb. I've just given voice to a black, malignant thought that's been growing in my mind. Or, is this Hecate's divine, and most difficult, prophetic call to die to motherhood? Oh, to commit the crime of crimes – Never shall I consider the slaughter of my own sweet, innocent children, my own flesh and blood. But, neither can I yield them up to the Corinthians, my spiteful enemies, allowing hands less merciful than mine to extinguish their breath, and surely death is the inevitable penance for the mortal deed of eradicating a royal house.

Does the act upon which I now meditate, belong to an intention and purpose that transcends all human plans and designs. Is the sin of sins really an essential cog in the wheel of providence, and thus no sin at all? For the Moira's dominion extends far beyond the control of the most powerful male gods, determining no less than the entire course of human destiny. At such times, is it not best to resign to that which is destined, or inevitably decreed, and acknowledge human reason's inability to comprehend certain matters, matters of faith, plain and simple? Is it not appropriate to place our unconditional trust in the omniscient, inexplicable powers which are beyond the limited scope of our comprehension, beyond any and all reasoned argument?

Be courageous, my heart, and shrink not from this fated task. Forget how dear they are to you, and more, forget that they are yours, if only for one short hour, and then, allow their souls to be ennobled in heaven for all eternity!

Shall I do it? Oh, why my soul, do you waiver? My heart vacillates, it pulls me in two directions simultaneously. Hera, I too am strung out between the time of heaven and humanity, the burdensome weight of maternal obligation works to hold me fast to the earth, while the call of the immortals, beckoning from the beyond, stretches me skyward. However, this transcends the internal battle of reason against the passions, where renouncing reason produces an animal, and renouncing the passions begets a god.

(Long pause)

What a paradox we all are unto ourselves. Humble yourself weak reason, be silent foolish passion, and submit to faith's superior yoke. Humanity infinitely transcends itself, and to learn of our true condition, we must attune ourselves to the voices of divinity! As Hecate prophesied, in order to emblazon the night sky with my name everlasting, it is with my own hand that I must seize immortality, and in the process, perhaps, justice will at last be served. I must burn brightly like a flame from heaven, I am the flame from heaven. I gave birth to the children, it is therefore my duty – to perform the ultimate sacrifice, which will at once set the cosmos to circle back upon itself.It is Hecate's will that I should destroy this world, a world in disarray, for the things once esteemed above all others are now devalued, and what a pitiless world it is that forces a mother and her offspring into poverty and exile! I am not heartless, but rather it is the world which I inhabit that lacks faith, heart, and compassion.

Nurse:

Oh, gods, the children are forever lost to their mother...

Medea:

> *(Turns to Nurse with resolve)*

No, never are they dead to their mother, because they are promised to heaven! It is to Jason, their father, that they will forever be lost!

> *(The Pedagogue approaches Medea with the two children while a Messenger from the palace of Creon is running toward the house, shouting from a distance and waving his arms about.)*

Get the children in the house now!

Pedagogue:

I have good news, my lady – because of the gifts, peace exists. Why the distressed looks with these good tidings?

Nurse:

You have no idea what is going on!
Get inside!

> *(The confused Pedagogue moves past the women into the house.)*

Medea: *(Aside to Nurse)*

Go within and prepare what is needed for this, the final hour.

> *(The Nurse glares at Medea in recalcitrance and then goes into the house. Enter Messenger, screaming as he comes on the scene.)*

Messenger:

Ruin, total ruin! Our royalty is annihilated. Daughter and father have fallen to fits and paroxysm! Run, Medea, flee, for your life! Creon and Creusa are dead, killed by your poisonous drugs.

Medea:

What glorious news you bring! I shall forever be in your debt!

Messenger:

Are you mad?
Did you hear what I said?

Medea:

Of course I heard you, now elaborate and tell me everything, down to the smallest detail!

Messenger:

When your children arrived with the gifts an atmosphere of elation erupted within the house. Servants were hopeful that the feud between you and their new lord had come to a peaceful, agreeable ending. But, when Jason led the children into the princess's chambers, she became upset to see the little boys with their father. But her mood was quickly assuaged when she noticed that the children carried presents within their wicker-baskets. Her eyes lit up as she looked at Jason who said, "They have come with treasures for you, my love. Please accept these gifts from my children and in return, see it in your heart, to sway your father's decision to exile my children." Blushing, she shyly smiled at Jason, and spoke the smart words of a devoted bride, "I will always abide by your wishes, and immediately attend to your request. It is only right that a wife should honor her husband, embracing all the things that he holds dear." Then she proceeded to model her smart, newly acquired wardrobe. First, the tiara was placed upon her head. She playfully tossed and arranged the flowing locks of her black hair in the mirror, which an attendant held before her. Next, she was assisted into the long silky dress, which was fastened and wrapped tightly around her waist, and finally, the necklace, with sparkling golden medallions, was clasped around her delicate, white neck. She began to stroll confidently about the bedchamber, striking exaggerated poses. It was obvious that she greatly admired her youthful, slender physique, which was greatly accentuated and enhanced by the cut and flow of the perfectly fashioned gown. All at once, her beautiful mood turned ugly. Her body began to reverberate with uncontrolled muscular spasms, the pupils of her eyes rolled back in her head, and she started to foam at the mouth. The attendants immediately ran to fetch the king, who, upon arriving, screamed in horror and ran to her aid, calling urgently for assistance. But, all those present slowly backed away to the far corners of the room, believing that the girl was in the midst of Dionysian possession, as if the angered god, for what ever reason, had sent her into a violent fit of tormented mania. Sobbing uncontrollably, Creon reached out. In an attempt to comfort Creusa, with tear-filled eyes, he lamented, "Without my child I could never bear the brunt of existence." Then, as he attempted to cradle her in his arms, something even more horrible occurred! She began to strangle and crush the life from his body. He desperately attempted to free himself, striking out violently at her with all his might, but it was no use. He was no match for her ungodly strength. Then, after a moment, he too began to convulse, and they both screamed in agony and sank down.

Stretched supine on the cold marble of the palace floor, father and daughter expired as a grisly mass of tangled, contorted flesh.

Medea:

(To the Children)

Oh, my children, we must soon part ways! But, not in vain, did I suffer your birth. Although I will never adorn the beds of your brides, or stand with my torch at your weddings. And the plans I once had to be cared for by you as I age and die, have now changed, you shall not leave the earth in vain, nor will I suffer your death in vain!

(To Pedagogue)

Take yourself away, man.

(To the Women and Pedagogue)

If any present are unclean and unfit to attend this sacrifice, depart at once from this house, or avert your eyes.

Pedagogue:

(Weeping)

Spare the babes!

Medea:

No, the die is cast! My hand will not falter!

*(Medea forcefully drags the
children to the sacrificial altar.)*

Episode V

Choral Song:

No hope exists for the children's lives. Toward a
certain death they are headed. Such miseries do
we lament, but be courageous with unwavering
hand, Oh, sorrowful mother, who must slay your
offspring.

> *(Breaking the rhythm of the
> choral dance, the Priestesses
> address Hecate regarding
> the events that are about to
> transpire. They make a plea for
> the lives of the children.)*

Priestess #1:

> *(Removes mask and throws it to
> the ground)*

Wait, should we allow such a thing to happen? This
act seems the very opposite of just punishment,
for it appears in this case that the punishment
far exceeds the crime. How is it that such a

deed will ennoble womanhood and appease the immortals?

Priestess #2:

(Removes mask)

Oh, great Hecate, can you assure us that from this act, which on the surface appears so vile and heinous, a greater or equal evil will be prevented, that it will somehow benefit the state of the universe? Hecate, please speak...

Priestess #3:

(Removes mask)

Who should be asked to destroy with savage hand their own sons? What crime and sin is so egregious that it demands as punishment a mother's children, slaughtered by her own hand, no less? Blood for blood has been the way of things, but the blood of innocents, how can this truly be justified under any law, divine or not?   Must we kill to destroy evil doers? Is this not making two evil doers in place of one? Evil should be overcome with true justice! While right without might is helpless, might lacking right is heartless and tyrannical.

*(The Children's voices sound
from offstage.)*

Priestess #1:

> Listen, to those voices, Medea has not yet spilled the blood of the children. We must stop her before she defiles Mother Earth with the blood of those boys. Born of godly nobility, Medea now sets to defile all that the gods and humanity should hold sacred. Arrest her hand, Hecate, suffer her not to strike! Such a polluting curse will be hard to bear up. It cannot be so, that the three great mothers would ever desire such a senseless and violent form of recompense.

Priestess #2:

> It seems that such an abhorrent crime, sanctifies the ever widening circle of destruction, for as opposed to ending the cycle of violence, this act will in fact perpetuate it. Oh, I shudder to think of the three sisters who mercilessly avenge the spilling of kindred blood...they will not be deterred, for they possess an unholy blood-hunger, which is fed by insatiable vengeance. Nothing can halt or deter the Erinyes, born of the blood-castration of Uranus not even a god!

First Child:

> Mother, what are you doing? You're hurting me!

Priestess #4:

> *(Removes mask)*

Listen to those cries, there is still hope from death! We must bring help. You must stop this, Hecate! Are you as hard as she, harder than a rock of adamantine? You must tell us now, Hecate, what is it that the great mother goddesses desire. What is the just punishment in this case? What should we to do, we who are the holy priestesses in your divine service, Hecate? Tell us, or please allow us to stop the butchering of these babies!

> *(Hecate picks up a discarded mask, raising it to her face, she speaks.)*

Hecate:

As supernatural beings, we once enjoyed a glorious and resplendent existence, exercising our special power over mortal life and the course of Nature! Then came a time when we existed as do shadows in Hades. Now the eyes of Zeus no longer perceive the cosmos, they are as black and hollow as those of a tragic mask – a funeral mask! In truth, we are now dead to the world, the soul, and breadth of life, has left us...

Second Child:

No, Mother, no!

First Child:

Please no!

> *(Enter Jason on the scene. He
> stands outside the house.)*

Jason:

Where is she? Is she in the house, or has she already
fled? Creon's auxiliaries have been dispatched; I
must rescue my children before they are made to
pay with their blood for Medea's crimes!

> *(Pedagogue, covered in blood,
> runs out of the house and into
> Jason.)*

Pedagogue:

You poor soul, you know not what awaits you in
there. Medea's hands are drenched to the elbows
in the blood of your children!

Jason:

Oh, I shudder to see this unspeakable horror. I
will kill her, that she-beast!

> *(Medea slowly exits the house
> stained in blood, with dagger in
> hand.)*

Medea:

Why do you seek the dead in vain? The children
are now on their funeral pyre. I should take this

dagger, and before your eyes, plunge it into my stomach and cut out the last memories of your false promises.

> *(Medea slowly approaches Jason with dagger in hand, covered in blood.)*

Jason:

You accursed, abominable creature! How could you find the heart to stab the sons of your womb? What you have done is blight the sanctity of all that is holy. To have brought you forth from your savage barbarian home was the biggest mistake I have ever made. You killed your brother and betrayed your father. Why did I spurn the fair maidens of Greece for you, a Chimera or Scylla?

Medea:

The world knows what I suffered for you! It is you who have blighted the heavens and the sacred vows of matrimony when you deserted me. Did you think that the immortal goddesses would ignore such an abomination of Hera's law? Did you expect a life of bliss with your new whore of a bride? Did you really think that I would allow you to mock and turn me away? I am your one true wife! Creon, that old bastard, got what he rightly deserves for pandering his daughter and declaring my exile. Is there no thought for repercussion within your ways of logic?

Jason:

You are the one who should be concerned with the repercussion of these acts! By the gods, you'll pay the highest price for these inhuman acts! The Erinyes will mercilessly avenge this heinous spilling of kindred blood. In killing our children, you've caused yourself manifold and unthinkable pain as well!

Medea:

Not so, for it was not murder, it was a sacrifice sanctioned by all that is holy. Unlike you, I am most concerned with the children! Should they grow to maturity in a world such as this? From this day forward, they shall never suffer the wrongs which your sins have brought down, like a plague, upon this house! Worry not for their souls and think only of your own, for the children are now safe. And as for my pain, for all eternity, I will use your suffering and misery as a counterpoise, and this knowledge will perhaps ease my mind. And all the torturous, unbearable pains brought about by the all-to-human ties to the mortal earth, brought about by the fall from divine origins, will find their justification. I will transcend the mortal body, which strains to endure untold physical sufferings and the continuous onslaught of the passions, and the mortal mind, which desperately longs to soar skyward, endeavoring the unbridgeable distance between us and the truth of our wretched condition. But, as for you, sentenced and condemned to a life of infernal torment for your crimes, if you think that you weep now, wait until old age has ravaged your youth, then you'll learn the true meaning of pain and loss. Go now and bury your bride – call me what you like – I am a Scylla, Chimera – as well a Harpy and witch. Now I will surely live up to my reputation by feeding on your heart! Consider yourself justly paid, but this retribution has implications, which are far beyond your understanding, beyond any and all human comprehension!

> *(Medea moves to center stage.*
> *Light on Jason down. A single*
> *light illuminates Medea who*
> *directs her gaze upward.)*

Hecate, I await your arrival. In the name of Medea I have consecrated the process of cosmic justice. It is finished! And now the heavens will part,as the path opens for you and the baying hounds, submitted to your command. I shall now escape Corinth forever, and walk, with torch in hand, the lofty spaces of heaven with you…in the company of the divine.

> *(Medea concludes her plea to*
> *Hecate and remains in the light*
> *for an extended duration. Her*
> *confident anticipation gives way*

to a bewildered anxiety. She is silent and motionless. Hecate does not appear as the deus ex machina. The light on Medea slowly fades to black. Soft light up on Jason, kneeling with his head clutched in his hands.)

Jason:

Oh, my children, my poor, innocent children, to have such a mother...

(Long pause)

Now I must wash and clothe their bodies for burial, but there will be no funeral rites, no libations of wine and oil poured on the ground or rubbed on the corpses. Because from this day forward, I will never cease testifying to the cruel reality that no gods exist!

(Light dims. Stage goes black)

End.

www.ingramcontent.com/pod-product-compliance
Lightning Source LLC
Chambersburg PA
CBHW031326060726
47590CB00003B/1349